Amelia Bedelia

& FRIENDS

Beat the Clock

me →

by Herman Parish

pictures by Lynne Avril

Greenwillow Books
An Imprint of HarperCollins Publishers

Art was created digitally in Adobe Photoshop.

Amelia Bedelia is a registered trademark of Peppermint Partners, LLC.

Amelia Bedelia & Friends Beat the Clock. Text copyright © 2019 by Herman S. Parish III. Illustrations copyright © 2019 by Lynne Avril. All rights reserved. No part of this book may be used or reproduced in any manner whatsoever without written permission except in the case of brief quotations embodied in critical articles and reviews. Printed in the United States of America. For information address HarperCollins Children's Books, a division of HarperCollins Publishers, 195 Broadway, New York, NY 10007. www.harpercollinschildrens.com

Library of Congress Control Number: 2019944437

ISBN 9780062935182 (hardback) — ISBN 9780062961815 (paper-over-board) —
ISBN 9780062935175 (paperback)

19 20 21 22 23 PC/LSCC 10 9 8 7 6 5 4 3 2 1 First Edition

Greenwillow Books

For Yumiko,
whose friendship stands the test of time!
—H. P.

For Keely and Nika, with love!
—L. A.

Amelia Bedelia

Finally

Joy

Heather

Clay

Cliff

Wade

Dawn

Skip

Angel

Penny

Contents

Chapter 1

Choosing Sides— Good and Bad

Crunch! CRUNCH!! KAY-RUNCH!!!

Amelia Bedelia's feet were talking to her. They were saying that she was walking under a giant oak tree laden with acorns. She closed her eyes and kept walking, listening to acorns being crushed under her sneakers with every step she took.

CRUNcrunch! CrUNch! K-K-runch!

UNCH!
K-K-RUNCH   CRUNCH!
K-K-runch   CRUNCH! K-K-RUNCH

1

Amelia Bedelia imagined that if acorns could talk, they were probably saying "Welcome to Oak Tree Elementary!"

The oak tree in front of her school was as old as it was enormous. Its leaves were just beginning to turn brown, a dusty brown that made the whole tree look like it had been sprinkled with cocoa powder.

"BOO!!!" hollered Clay. Amelia Bedelia jumped and opened her eyes. Her friend Clay had snuck up behind her.

"You look like you're sleepwalking," said Clay, laughing.

"Who can sleep through this racket?" said Amelia Bedelia. She *crunch!* jumped into the air and landed *K-K-RUNCH* *CRUNCH! K-K-RUNCH* on some acorns. Clay covered his ears with his hands.

"This tree is making acorns like that's its job," said Clay.

"Well, I guess making acorns *is* its job," said Amelia Bedelia. "This tree doesn't have to practice the piano or learn how to speak Spanish or memorize multiplication tables or do word problems. The only thing our oak tree has to do is make acorns."

"It's doing an awesome job of that,"

said Clay. "There are millions of them!"

"Right!" said Amelia Bedelia. "Like our school motto says . . ."

"Mighty oaks from little acorns grow!" chanted Amelia Bedelia and Clay together.

They said good morning to Ms. Hotchkiss and Mrs. Roman as they passed the school office. Ms. Hotchkiss was the principal, but Mrs. Roman, her assistant, really ran the school. Everyone knew that, even Ms. Hotchkiss.

"I like your necklace, Mrs. Roman," said Clay.

"Thank you, Clay. You're very thoughtful," said Mrs. Roman, smiling.

Clay whispered to Amelia Bedelia. "I always give Mrs. Roman a compliment. You never want to be on her bad side."

Amelia Bedelia turned around to look at Mrs. Roman. Her left side looked the same as her right side. Amelia Bedelia did not see a bad side. She was about to ask Clay what he meant when Mrs. Shauk greeted them at the door to their classroom.

"How nice of you two to honor us with your presence," said Mrs. Shauk. She watched them take their seats, living up to her unofficial nickname—the Hawk.

A second later, Ms. Hotchkiss read the morning announcements over the intercom. "Good morning, everyone! This is a reminder that next week we will be celebrating the one hundredth birthday of Oak Tree Elementary, so get ready! There will be lots of food and fun—and music, games, and activities for all. Make sure you thank your parents and teachers for all the work they have put into making this event a success!"

Ms. Hotchkiss passed the microphone to Mrs. Roman. Mrs. Roman was

in charge of finding out trivia about the school to build interest for the hundredth-birthday celebration. "Here is today's fun fact about Oak Tree Elementary," said Mrs. Roman. "Did you know that it takes an oak tree twenty to thirty years to start producing acorns?"

Then Mrs. Roman read the day's cafeteria menu. Cheers and clapping erupted when Mrs. Roman announced that pizza was for lunch.

MENU

Clap
Clap!

Clap

"My dad says that Romans make the best pizza," said Clay. "Now *that* is a fun fact!"

"Mrs. Roman only *said* pizza," said Amelia Bedelia. "She did not make the pizza, and she is not a Roman."

"I like to give her all the credit, to stay on her good side," explained Clay.

Amelia Bedelia shrugged and looked out the classroom window. She had a great view of the giant oak tree that gave their school its name. She loved watching the seasons change as the leaves turned, then blew away, only to pop out again in spring. Mrs. Shauk had once told Amelia Bedelia

that she had the best seat in the house.

"This is my school, not my house," Amelia Bedelia had replied. "But I definitely have the best view!"

Chapter 2

One Year x One Hundred = Centennial

During the announcements, Mrs. Shauk had been busy writing on the board. After the applause for pizza died down, she pointed at what she had written and asked, "Has anyone seen these letters around the school?"

MCMXX

"Is this another language or English?" asked Pat. "That doesn't look like an English word to me."

"You're right," said Mrs. Shauk. "It's Latin."

"Like they speak in Latin America?" said Heather.

"No . . . Spanish, Portuguese, and other languages are spoken in Latin America. This is Latin like they spoke in ancient Rome," said Mrs. Shauk. "Today, Latin is a dead language."

"Is that what zombies speak?" asked Pat.

"Zombies don't speak. That's why they are zombies," said Penny.

11

"These letters stand for numbers called Roman numerals," said Mrs. Shauk.

Clay was nodding at Amelia Bedelia. She could tell what he was thinking— that Mrs. Roman was so important she even had her own numbers.

"You people walk right by these letters twice a day," said Mrs. Shauk.

Joy raised her hand. "Oh, I know, I know!" she said. "They're carved on the stone near the front door."

"That's right. You're very observant, Joy," said Mrs. Shauk. "The letters were carved into a stone block

called the cornerstone. The corner[stone]
was the first thing the builders who bu[ilt]
our school put in place. All of the other
stone blocks and bricks were built
after it."

"Is it like when people put
letters and numbers on license
plates to spell out a joke?" asked Angel.

"Like L-A-10 S E-Z," said Clay.

"Yeah," said Cliff. "Latin is easy,"

"You guys, E-N-F S E-N-F,"
said Mrs. Shauk.

They thought about that for a second.

Then they nodded.

"OK," said Cliff.

"I C," said Clay.

"C D B," said Joy.

Mrs. Shauk. "The builder
man numerals to record
ding was built."

was MCMXX?"
asked Heather.

"Reading Roman numerals is like
breaking a code," said Mrs. Shauk.

"So the letters are numbers and
the numbers are letters?" asked
Amelia Bedelia.

"Exactly, Amelia Bedelia!" said
Mrs. Shauk. "The letter M stands for
the number one thousand. The letter X is
ten. Now what if you have two Ms and
two Xs?"

"That's two thousand plus twenty,"
said Dawn.

"That's this year—2020!" said Rose.

"That's right," said Mrs. Shauk. "The year 2020 is written MMXX in Roman numerals."

"But our cornerstone has a C between the two Ms," said Joy.

Wow, thought Amelia Bedelia. Mrs. Shauk was right about Joy. She definitely saw things that most people didn't notice.

"Good point!" said Mrs. Shauk. "Well, the letter C comes from the Latin word *cent*, which means one hundred. That's where we get the word *century*, which means one hundred years. And a cent is one hundredth of a dollar."

"Our class has our very own cent," said Amelia Bedelia. "Her name is Penny."

Amelia Bedelia grabbed Penny by the wrist, pulling her to her feet to take a bow.

"The rule with Roman numerals is that putting a letter in front of another one subtracts that amount," said Mrs. Shauk. "So, putting a C in front of an M subtracts one hundred from one thousand."

"That makes nine hundred," said Joy. "The first M is one thousand and the second is nine hundred. So, the year is 1900, plus twenty makes it 1920. And you write it MCMXX."

"And that is why we are having a

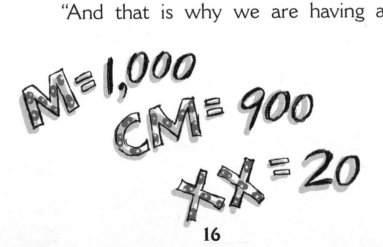

M = 1,000
CM = 900
XX = 20

centennial celebration!" said Mrs. Shauk.

"A centennial is a celebration that happens every hundred years," said Heather. "My great-grandmother just had hers!"

"*Centennial* comes from Latin, too," said Mrs. Shauk.

"For a dead language, Latin sure keeps popping up," said Amelia Bedelia.

"Latin *must* be a zombie language," said Cliff. "It refuses to die!"

"Why didn't the ancient Romans just use regular numbers?" asked Chip.

"I think Roman numerals look older and more important," said Holly.

"Expensive watches use Roman numerals," said Mrs. Shauk. "Some

people think it makes them look more elegant."

"Roman numerals are fun," said Clay.

"If I gave you a quiz on them, would you get one hundred percent?" asked Mrs. Shauk.

"Yup! Because *percent* is Latin," said Clay.

Amelia Bedelia was raising her hand to ask about percentages when the Voice of Doom came over the intercom.

"Mrs. Shauk, I still need an attendance report from you," said Mrs. Roman.

Amelia Bedelia froze with her hand still up in the air. Even Mrs. Shauk was so startled that she jumped.

"Oh, thanks for volunteering, Amelia Bedelia," said Mrs. Shauk, writing down the attendance number on a slip of paper and handing it to Amelia Bedelia. "Let's see if Mrs. Roman lives up to her name."

Amelia Bedelia shrugged. She hadn't meant to volunteer, but it was always fun to be sent on a mission during class.

When she passed Clay on the way out, he caught her arm and whispered, "You lucky duck! Just remember, Mrs. Roman probably invented those numbers, so stay on her good side."

"Quack!" said Amelia Bedelia with a laugh.

Chapter 3

"Watch It . . . Watch It!"

Amelia Bedelia waddled as fast as she could down the hall. When she was sure that no one was looking, she started running. By the time she got to the office, she was out of breath.

"My goodness, Amelia Bedelia," said Ms. Hotchkiss. "Even I can walk to your classroom without getting winded."

Mrs. Roman's eyes narrowed to slits. "Amelia Bedelia, you did walk here, correct?" she said.

Amelia Bedelia couldn't catch her breath. Finally she nodded and handed Mrs. Roman the piece of paper that Mrs. Shauk had given her.

Mrs. Roman opened the attendance report. She turned it around and around and finally turned it upside down. Frowning, she looked at Amelia Bedelia.

"Is this a joke, Amelia Bedelia?" asked Mrs. Roman. "What kind of number is this?"

Uh-oh, thought Amelia Bedelia. It

looked like when Mrs. Roman was unhappy, her bad side was her front! Mrs. Roman was still squinting at Amelia Bedelia and shaking her head back and forth when Ms. Hotchkiss took the piece of paper from her.

Ms. Hotchkiss laughed. "Would you read this for Mrs. Roman, Amelia Bedelia?" she asked.

"XX is twenty, plus V is five, and II is two, which equals twenty-seven," said Amelia Bedelia.

"Perfect," said Ms. Hotchkiss. "And perfect attendance. You should study your Roman numerals, Mrs. Roman."

"Mrs. Shauk wondered if you would live up to your name," said Amelia Bedelia.

"Oh, she did, did she?" said Mrs. Roman.

"Yup! And Clay said you had invented Roman numerals and named them after yourself," said Amelia Bedelia.

Ms. Hotchkiss laughed again.

"Sounds like Clay is trying to get on my bad side," said Mrs. Roman.

Oh, no, thought Amelia Bedelia. She had wanted to stay on Mrs. Roman's good side. Now she was on her bad side, dragging Mrs. Shauk and Clay along with her. If she made Mrs. Roman mad at Clay, Amelia Bedelia would not be a lucky duck in his eyes. She would be a dead duck.

"Oh, Clay never wants to be on your bad side," said Amelia Bedelia. "But I don't think you have a bad side. Your front, back, and both sides all look good to me."

"Thank you so much," said Mrs. Roman, smiling. "That's very nice of you."

"Don't thank me yet," said Mr. Jack, the school's custodian, as he walked into the office. Mr. Jack went by his first name because he said he was a jack-of-all-trades. "Wait until I finish your job. I put the easel in the lobby. Now, which picture do you want moved out there?"

"The one on the wall behind the counter," said Ms. Hotchkiss. "It was the first photograph of the students and teachers of

Oak Tree Elementary, taken in 1920." She pointed at a large, framed black-and-white photograph.

Amelia Bedelia had always wondered who the people in the photograph were. She had been in the office lots of times but had never had the chance to ask. "Is that really our school?" she said.

"You bet, Amelia Bedelia. Look right here," said Mrs. Roman, pointing to

a little tree in the foreground. "This little sapling grew up to be the giant oak tree out front."

"It's a really big picture," said Amelia Bedelia. "They must have used a huge camera."

"The original picture was small. I'm sure they blew it up," said Ms. Hotchkiss.

"Really?" said Amelia Bedelia. "They blew it up?"

"They enlarged it as much as possible," said Mrs. Roman. "Need any help, Mr. Jack?"

"I'll try it single-handedly, but this thing is heavier than it looks," Mr. Jack said.

It must be heavy, thought

Amelia Bedelia. Mr. Jack was using both of his hands to lift it, carrying it double-handedly. She was standing between Mr. Jack and the office door. She was about to move out of the way when Mr. Jack asked for her help.

"Watch it . . . watch it!" said Mr. Jack, walking toward Amelia Bedelia with the huge framed photo. He seemed to be having some trouble seeing where he

was going. "Watch it!" he said to Amelia Bedelia again.

As usual, Amelia Bedelia did what she was told. She watched the framed picture. She did not move at all.

BAMMMM!

BAMMMM! The frame crashed into the counter. Mr. Jack set the photograph down on the floor, leaning it against the front of the counter.

"I was asking Amelia Bedelia to be careful and move out of my way," he explained, looking embarrassed.

"That's okay. It was an

accident," said Ms. Hotchkiss.

"Accidents happen," said Mrs. Roman.

Amelia Bedelia was relieved. She must be on Mrs. Roman's good side after all. That was when Amelia Bedelia spied the envelope that had fallen to the floor when the framed photograph hit the counter. She picked it up. It was addressed to "The Principal" in beautiful cursive handwriting. She handed it to Ms. Hotchkiss.

"What's this for?" said Ms. Hotchkiss.

"It's for the principal. That's you," said Amelia Bedelia. "It's written in cursive writing."

"Cursive writing is becoming a lost art, like Roman numerals," said Mrs. Roman.

"But where did this envelope come

Cursive writing

from?" asked Ms. Hotchkiss.

"From the photo," said Amelia Bedelia. "Mr. Jack was telling me to 'Watch it, watch it,' and I was watching it, and I saw the envelope fall onto the floor when the picture frame banged the counter."

Mrs. Roman took the envelope from Ms. Hotchkiss. She used a sharp letter opener to slit open the top edge. "It would be a shame to tear into an envelope this pretty," she said. "Someone took a lot of trouble to make it look so nice." She handed it back to Ms. Hotchkiss, who just kept staring down at it.

"I can't stand the suspense!" said Mrs. Roman. "Would you like me to read it for you?"

The Principal

"Thank you, but I can do it. It's addressed to me, after all," said Ms. Hotchkiss. "I'm just surprised! And I do love a mystery."

She pulled the letter out of the envelope and unfolded it. It was written in the same fancy cursive writing.

Amelia Bedelia noticed that Ms. Hotchkiss was moving her lips as she read silently.

"Oh, my," Ms. Hotchkiss said, looking up at them. Then she kept reading.

"What does it say?" asked Mrs. Roman.

"My, my," said Ms. Hotchkiss.

"Is that all it says?" asked Amelia Bedelia.

After she'd read a little bit more, Ms. Hotchkiss looked up again. "Oh, my goodness," she said, then went back to reading.

"Is it a bill? Is something broken? Did something flood?" asked Mr. Jack.

"Oh, my goodness gracious," said Ms. Hotchkiss. She handed the note to Mrs. Roman. "Read it yourself. Read it to everyone. That picture hitting the counter was no accident!"

NEWS

Chapter 4
Breaking News!

Since Mrs. Roman hadn't had the chance to read the note yet, she began by reading it to herself. "This is incredible," she said.

Then she went back to the beginning to read it out loud. She held it up, pointing at the date in the upper right-hand corner. "This letter is dated October, 1920," she said. Then she began.

October 1st, 1920.

I write this letter in the year 1920. My name is Peter Hoffman. I am the first principal of our town's new school, Oak Tree Elementary. Our town has plenty of monuments, statues, and plaques that celebrate the noble achievements of our citizens. We would also like to celebrate the students who pass through the doors of our school. To honor the lives of ordinary citizens, we have gathered an assortment of everyday objects from daily life in our town. We want to give future generations an idea of how we worked and played and thought and felt. We have collected these items in a time capsule, to be opened one hundred years from now, in the year 2020. You will find it buried at the base of the old oak tree, in the direction of true north.

Good luck! Be well and prosper!

I remain your humble servant,

Peter C. Hoffman

"Isn't this incredible?"
said Ms. Hotchkiss. "Here we are, about
to celebrate our school's one hundredth
birthday, when a letter about a centennial
time capsule falls in our lap!"

"It fell on the floor first,"
said Amelia Bedelia.

"Now all we have to do is find that time
capsule before the party," said Mrs. Roman.

"Well, we've got five days to beat the
clock," said Ms. Hotchkiss. "Mrs. Roman,
I am putting you in charge!"

"Here's the first thing we
should do," said Mrs. Roman.
"Let's get the whole school
involved. We'll make an announcement
about the time capsule. I'll tell the story of

what happened in this office today, and Amelia Bedelia can read Principal Hoffman's letter to everyone."

Ms. Hotchkiss, Mrs. Roman, and Amelia Bedelia gathered around the microphone.

"Sounds like a good plan," said Ms. Hotchkiss. "Mr. Jack, we may need a shovel."

"Attention! This is your principal," said Ms. Hotchkiss into the mic. "I'm sorry to interrupt your work, but we have some important breaking news—"

SMASH! Tinkle-plinkity-plink . . .

In his hurry, Mr. Jack had snagged his foot on the picture frame. The whole thing fell over and hit the floor hard, shattering the glass. They could barely look at one another without bursting out laughing.

"I'll go get a broom, too," said Mr. Jack, shaking his head.

Ms. Hotchkiss gestured for Mrs. Roman to take over. Finally Mrs. Roman stopped laughing long enough to tell the students of Oak Tree Elementary about the accident that had led to the discovery of the letter, and to introduce Amelia Bedelia. Amelia Bedelia stepped up to the microphone.

"I would like to read you a letter written one hundred years ago,"

39

said Amelia Bedelia. Then she stopped. It wasn't because she had said such a strange thing. Although it was strange to think of reading a message that had taken a century to reach them rather than a minute or even a second. . . . No, she was feeling weird just hearing the sound of her own voice.

Of course she heard herself speak every day. But now she was imagining her voice echoing down the halls, rebounding off lockers, and bouncing off bulletin boards, through the gym and cafeteria and library into every classroom in the school, including her own. She wondered what her friends were thinking. Were they wondering what had happened to her? She was only supposed to deliver the attendance record, but she'd been gone a long time. Did her voice sound funny? Did they think she sounded like herself? Were they paying attention?

Finally she read the letter.

"I write this letter in the year 1920. My name is Peter Hoffman. I am the first principal of our town's new school, Oak Tree Elementary. Our town has plenty of monuments, statues, and plaques that celebrate the noble achievements of our citizens. We would also like to celebrate the students who pass through the doors of our school. To honor the lives of ordinary citizens, we have gathered an assortment of everyday objects from daily life in our town. We want to give future generations an idea of how we worked and played and thought and felt. We have collected these items in a time capsule, to be opened one hundred years from now, in the year 2020. You will find it buried at the base of the old oak tree, in the direction of true north.

Good luck! Be well and prosper!

I remain your humble servant,

Peter C. Hoffman"

On her way back to class, Amelia Bedelia sensed a surge of excitement flowing through the school, as though someone had switched on an electric current. When she got back to her room, she was a celebrity. Her friends and classmates gathered around to ask her questions.

Q: Was that you on the intercom?

A: Yes.

Q: Are you famous?

A: No.

Q: Is it true that you saw the letter first?

A: Yes.

Q: Can I have your autograph?

A: Sure.

Mrs. Shauk had wasted no time. She had written TIME CAPSULE on the board. She asked Angel to look up the term in the dictionary and to read the definition out loud.

"A container holding historical records or objects representative of current culture that is deposited (as in the earth or in a cornerstone) for preservation until discovery by some future age," read Angel.

Amelia Bedelia hardly ever thought about the past or the future. She liked to focus on the here and now. And right this minute she wanted to find that hundred-year-old time capsule, open it up, and discover what was inside!

Chapter 5

Cracked Up to Be

That night, after her homework, Amelia Bedelia and her parents sat down to supper. It looked delicious, as always. Amelia Bedelia knew that the news of her day would change her life. She was savoring the feeling of anticipation, making sure she would be able to remember what their lives were like before the time capsule.

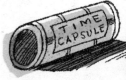

"Anything earth-shattering happen in school today?" asked her father.

"The earth was okay," said Amelia Bedelia. "It was a glass-shattering day."

Then she told them about the Roman numerals, taking **XXVII** the attendance report to the office, Mrs. Roman's sides, Mr. Jack moving the framed photograph, watching it but not watching it, the picture dropping and the glass shattering, discovering a note from one hundred years ago, then announcing that news to the whole school and becoming a celebrity.

Amelia Bedelia was halfway through her

story when she noticed that her parents had stopped eating. They were leaning toward her, their eyes wide, listening as hard as they could. When she finished, Amelia Bedelia took her first bite of lasagna.

"Delicious, Mom!" said Amelia Bedelia. Her parents were still stunned by her story. They looked at each other, then back at her.

"All that went on before lunch, sweetie?" said her mother.

"Every bit. The afternoon was much calmer," said Amelia Bedelia.

"Thank goodness. If I had gone through all that, I would have come home for a nap," said her father.

"Wow, that is incredible. What's next?" asked her mother.

"Ms. Hotchkiss wants to dig up the time capsule," said Amelia Bedelia. "She wants to display it at our centennial celebration."

"What fun!" said her mother.

"That would be a huge a feather in her cap."

Amelia Bedelia thought

49

that getting to see Ms. Hotchkiss wearing a cap with an enormous feather in it was even more reason to find that time capsule!

"When they find it, it will be interesting to see what the teachers and students in 1920 put inside to share with the teachers and students in 2020," said her mother.

"There are time capsules in existence that won't be opened for thousands of years," said her father.

"Thousands of years!" said Amelia Bedelia. "Nothing lasts that long. Who is going to remember where they buried it?"

"Well, when explorers discover

an ancient tomb, like those in Egypt, it's sort of a time capsule. Sometimes they find jewelry and furniture and scrolls, along with combs and mirrors and games and other stuff. Since those things are more than 4,000 years old, a tomb can be a time capsule of sorts."

Amelia Bedelia shook her head. "I can't imagine waiting 4,000 years for something. Christmas comes once a year, but it feels like it takes forever to get here. Grandma says that Christmas comes quicker for her every year, which is weird."

"Time is relative," said her mother.

"A relative like Grandma?" asked Amelia Bedelia.

"No, sweetie," said her father. "Relative

like 'compared to something else.' Grandma has seen way more Christmases than you. No matter what age you are, there are always three hundred and sixty-five days between Christmases every year. But as you get older, it sometimes feels as though it comes sooner and sooner. And when you are younger, it feels like it takes forever!"

"Sooner or later, the future is coming. Ready or not!" said her mother.

"When it comes to the future, there is only one thing you can be sure of. It never turns out quite like they say it will," said her father. "According to the magazines I

read when I was your age,
we should have a small helicopter in
our driveway instead of a car."

"Flying to school in a helicopter?
Cool!" said Amelia Bedelia.

"And you," continued her dad, "would
be zooming around with your jet pack
instead of riding your bike."

"Can I get one for my birthday?" asked
Amelia Bedelia, even though that day felt
like it was a really long time away.

"Sure, right after I get my helicopter,"
said her father.

"I can remember scientists saying that
no one would have to cook anymore,"

 said her mother. "A
whole meal would

be contained in one tiny pill."

"That does not sound delicious at all," said Amelia Bedelia.

"That's probably why it never caught on," said her father, standing up to clear the table. "The only good thing about taking a pill instead of cooking and eating is not having any dishes to do."

Amelia Bedelia joined her father at the sink, drying what he washed. "Then we'd have more time to race around with our jet packs," she said.

Chapter 6

Barking Up
the Wrong Tree

The next morning, hordes of kids descended on Oak Tree Elementary. At drop-off, students hurried out of cars or raced off buses and headed straight for the big oak tree out front. They carried every

type of tool used for digging. There were all sorts of shovels and spades and spoons, garden forks, hoes, and even a tiny toy trowel. The kids went right to work, competing to see who could dig the deepest and fastest.

Mrs. Roman was in the school office when she first got wind of what was happening out front. A mail carrier who had stopped in to deliver the mail said, "What a great idea to plant a garden out front so everyone can enjoy it!"

"Planting a what where?" asked Mrs. Roman.

"Under the big oak! I have never seen kids so excited about digging!"

Mrs. Roman ran out of the building. "What in the world?" she said, shaking her head.

Students were laughing and chatting while flinging dirt everywhere. It looked like fifty dogs were trying to bury their bones at the same time. The old plaque engraved with the school motto and the date 1921 had been dug up and was lying on a big pile of dirt.

Just then, Miss Chase, the gym teacher, jogged by. Mrs. Roman grabbed the whistle from around Miss Chase's neck and blew it with all her might.

TWWWWWWEEEEEEET!!!

The students froze.

"Are you guys woodchucks, or what?" yelled Mrs. Roman. "What do you think you're doing?"

"We're looking for the time capsule," said a boy in second grade.

"For Ms. Hotchkiss," said a girl in first grade.

"Well, she wouldn't want you hurting our oak tree or yourselves trying to find it," said Mrs. Roman. "This tree is big and strong. But if you disturb its roots, you could damage it. You don't want to go to school at Dead Oak Tree Elementary, do you? Fill up your holes and get to your classrooms, pronto!"

Amelia Bedelia leaned on her shovel until Mrs. Roman went back inside.

"Is she gone yet?" asked Clay, peeking out from behind Amelia Bedelia.

"Yes, Mrs. Roman is gone, you chicken," said Cliff, shaking his head and pushing dirt back into their hole.

"Clay isn't a chicken," said Amelia Bedelia.

"Or a duck or a

goose. He's our friend."

"Right!" said Joy. "One hundred percent."

"I hereby promote Clay to the level of a turkey, but no higher," said Cliff. "You can't go through school being afraid of Mrs. Roman."

Amelia Bedelia and her friends stopped by the bathrooms to wash off the dirt before heading to their classroom. They made it just in time for the morning announcements and a special message from Ms. Hotchkiss.

"Thanks to all of you who wanted to help locate the time capsule we learned about yesterday! We appreciate your enthusiasm. This afternoon, you may see workers around the tree using tools and equipment to locate the time capsule without harming our oak. It's an exciting project, and I will let you know as soon as they find something!"

Ms. Hotchkiss passed the microphone to Mrs. Roman. "Here is our fun fact for today," said Mrs. Roman. "When our school opened in 1920, fifty percent of the families in our town lived on farms."

"Wow!" said Clay. "She finally dug up a cool fact!"

After lunch, Amelia Bedelia and her

friends gathered out back at the student lounge near the playground. Unlike the teachers' lounge, which they imagined had comfortable chairs, snacks, and a television, the student lounge just had one piece of furniture. It was an old tree stump that had been turned into a table. The stump was nearly three feet in diameter and about a foot high.

Clay's father was a furniture maker, and he had helped the kids turn the stump into a table. He had trimmed off the part that was old and rotten. He showed them how to use sandpaper to smooth down the top. Then they painted it with varnish to protect it from the weather. The varnish dried hard and clear, and they could count the growth rings, one per year. It must have been a very old tree. When the bell rang, they headed back to their classroom for math.

Amelia Bedelia gazed out the window, distracted from her word problem by the team of workers taking measurements and pushing and pulling long metal rods in and out of the ground. One man was even using a metal detector, the kind she and her cousin Jason had seen treasure hunters using at the shore during the summer.

A few minutes later, Ms. Hotchkiss approached the workers. From the way they were all shaking their heads, Amelia Bedelia could tell they hadn't found anything. They loaded their equipment back into their truck and waved as Ms. Hotchkiss walked back inside.

Now what? thought Amelia Bedelia. Time was running out.

Chapter 7

Tempus ~~Fugit~~
Fuhgeddaboudit

Amelia Bedelia had promised to bring Pete, the owner of Pete's Diner, four dozen lemon tarts for his customers. She stopped by to make the delivery after school.

"Your tarts are the hottest item on the menu," said Doris, a waitress at the diner.

"Oh, you don't have to heat them up," said Amelia Bedelia.

"Well, they are popular, no matter what temperature," said Doris.

"I won't be able to make another delivery for a while," said Amelia Bedelia. "I'll be busy making lots of lemon tarts for my school's birthday."

"You go to Oak Tree Elementary, right?" asked Pete.

"I sure do," said Amelia Bedelia.

"I went there too," said Pete, holding out his hand.

Amelia Bedelia shook Pete's hand.

"In fact, my great-grandfather was the first principal," said Pete.

"You mean Peter Hoffman?" asked Amelia Bedelia.

Pete was stunned. "How did you know that?" he asked. "I was named after him. My mother loved telling stories about my great-grandfather. He loved gardening and trees. She told me that he always felt bad when the big old oak tree out behind the school died. It was huge! Ancient. He planted a new one out front, grown from an acorn off the old one."

"What else do you remember about him, Pete?" asked Doris, cutting a little slice of lemon tart to taste.

"I remember my mother telling me about his pocket watch," said Pete. "He would let her press a button, and the cover would flip open. She liked the face of the clock because it had big Roman numerals on it. The words 'Tempus fugit' were engraved on the inside."

"Is that who made the watch?" asked Amelia Bedelia.

"No. Tempus fugit means 'Time flies' in Latin," said Pete. "Way back when I was growing up, we all had to take Latin."

"You grew up speaking Latin?" said Amelia Bedelia. "Wow, you are much older than I thought. Did your mom and dad take you to the Colosseum to see the chariot races?"

It took a long time for Doris to stop laughing. She was still giggling when she put a plate of french fries in front of Amelia Bedelia.

"These are on the house," said Doris. "And if Julius Caesar . . . I mean Pete . . . doesn't agree, I'll pay for them. I needed

a good laugh today." Doris walked away,
wiping her eyes on her apron.

Amelia Bedelia didn't know
how french fries could be on the
house, especially when she was in
a diner, but she ate them all up anyway.
"These are hot and delicious!" she called
after Doris. "Thanks!"

Chapter 8

Stumped

There were only two days left until Oak Tree Elementary's official one hundredth birthday. Ms. Hotchkiss updated everyone on the search for the time capsule during morning announcements.

"We hired some experts to help us find the time capsule. You've probably noticed them as they searched

the area around our oak tree. They tell me that they used cutting-edge equipment. I am very sorry to tell you that they struck out."

Struck out? Amelia Bedelia wondered why the experts were playing baseball when they should have been hunting for that time capsule. Also, what edge was the equipment cutting?

"We are stumped!" added Mrs. Roman.

Too bad they weren't looking for a stump, thought Amelia Bedelia. She knew right where to find one.

After lunch, a gloomy bunch of kids gathered in the student lounge.

"Guess what? Our table is a year older than our oak tree," said Amelia Bedelia. She told her friends the story of Pete at the diner and Peter Hoffman, and how the tree in front of the school had been started from an acorn and planted when the tree that was now their table had died.

73

"According to the plaque next to the tree out front, it was planted in 1921," said Joy. Then she pointed to the edge of their table. "That means that this outer ring of our table was growing during the year 1920." The way she moved her fingers was like a tiny person walking toward the center of the stump, counting as she went.

1914 WWI

"Three, four, five, six. Right here is 1914. World War One started here," said Joy.

"There? I thought it was in Europe," said Amelia Bedelia.

Joy counted two more rings. "This would be the year 1912. The *Titanic* sank here."

"Sank there?" said Amelia Bedelia. "It's not deep enough. There is no water at all!"

The other kids fell over laughing, but not Joy.

"This is where the *Titanic* sank *in time*," said Joy. "See this ring? That is how big this tree was when the *Titanic* sank." Joy's fingers took twelve more teeny tiny steps toward the center of the stump. "Right here it's the year 1900," she said. "The turn of the last century. Want to keep going, back into the 1800s?"

"Sure!" said Amelia Bedelia and her friends.

"Lead on!" said Clay. "Your fingers are like little time travelers, walking back into history."

1876 Joy's fingers took more steps. "Here we are in 1876, when Alexander Graham Bell invented the telephone." Her fingers kept marching. She paused every so often to call out historical events, like stops on a train or bus.

Too soon, the recess bell rang and everyone started lining up to go in.

the first telephone

"Hurry, Joy," said Amelia Bedelia. "Go to the center ring and tell us what was going on when this tree was planted."

Walking her fingers as fast as she

could, Joy continued counting the years out loud and backward.

365 "This is 1865!" she called out. "The end of the Civil War!"

Civil War
cannon
1865

"Keep going!" said Amelia Bedelia as Joy's fingers did their dance. At last she got to the center of the stump.

1776 "1776!" Joy tapped the stump and smiled.

"The Declaration of Independence!" shouted Amelia Bedelia and her friends.

"Cool," said Clay. "All this time, we thought we were just sitting around an old stump. Turns out it's a slice of history. Thanks, Joy!"

Declaration of
Independence
1776

Back in the classroom, Clay explained to Mrs. Shauk and the other kids how Joy had turned the stump into a time machine. Joy was her usual self, sitting quietly at her desk with her nose in her book. She wasn't bragging. Which was what Amelia Bedelia liked most about her.

Joy loved discovering fun facts about the world. She was the absolute best at history. That was just a fact. Like the names and places and dates she had memorized. Those were a joy to her. Joy was a joy to Amelia Bedelia. She was super happy that Joy was her friend.

But right now, Amelia Bedelia could

78

tell that something was bothering Joy. Her forehead was wrinkled, and she stared off into the distance, studying the giant oak outside their classroom window.

Amelia Bedelia almost never passed notes in class, but she was worried enough to send one to Joy. Amelia Bedelia folded it up and passed it to Penny, who passed it to Clay, who passed it to Angel, who passed it to Joy. Amelia Bedelia saw Joy read it, write a reply, and send it back the same way.

Amelia Bedelia's note would have made the round trip in record time, in anyone else's classroom. But this was the home of the Hawk, and Mrs. Shauk had spotted the note immediately. She waited for Joy to answer it, then pounced right as it was being handed back to Amelia Bedelia. The blood-red talons of the Hawk snagged the note just before it got to Amelia Bedelia's outstretched hand. That note had as much chance as a baby bunny hopping across an open field at a raptor convention.

"Well, well, well. What do we have here?" asked Mrs. Shauk. "Is this perhaps the secret recipe for Amelia Bedelia's lemon tarts? It could not be merely a note, because everyone knows that those are one hundred percent banned in my class." Mrs. Shauk unfolded the paper and quickly read the message. "Joy and Amelia Bedelia, come to the front of the room, please."

The two friends stood up and slunk to the front of the room, then turned to face the class.

"This note started with you, Amelia Bedelia," said Mrs. Shauk. "Please tell us what was so important that you had to break my number-one rule." She dropped the note into Amelia Bedelia's outstretched palm, then took a seat at Amelia Bedelia's desk.

"I sent this to Joy," said Amelia Bedelia, "because she looked sad."

"And what does the note say?" said Mrs. Shauk.

Amelia Bedelia cleared her throat. "Are U OK?"

"Now please pass the note to Joy so she can share her reply with the entire class," said Mrs. Shauk.

"I wasn't feeling sad. I was thinking," said Joy. "I thought of something on the playground, and I just now figured it out."

"Could it be used as a fun fact?" asked Clay.

The whole class laughed. Mrs. Shauk laughed, too.

Thank goodness for Clay, thought Amelia Bedelia.

Joy turned the piece of paper over to read what she had written on the back. Amelia Bedelia perked up. She was looking forward to hearing the message she never got.

Joy cleared her throat twice and read, "I figured out where the time capsule is buried."

"Yes!" yelled Clay. "That's the funnest fact EVER!"

Mrs. Shauk's hawk-like eyes opened wide, then narrowed to slits. "I was going to send you both to the principal's office," she said. "But now I think Ms. Hotchkiss should come down here." She stood up, walked to the phone, and called the office. Everyone heard her say, "Hello, Mrs. Roman? Is Ms. Hotchkiss . . . ," before Mrs. Shauk turned her back to the class. She whispered for twenty seconds into the phone, then hung up.

Mrs. Shauk perched on the top of her desk. No one said one word. The only sound was two pairs of shoes walking quickly, never running, toward their classroom, growing louder and sharper with each *CLICK CLICKITY-CLACK CLICK CLACK!*

Chapter 9

Tempus Foundit

Mrs. Shauk's class, along with Ms. Hotchkiss and Mrs. Roman, assembled around the really old stump.

"Welcome to our student lounge," said Cliff. "I'd offer you something, but we don't have anything, except this really cool, really old stump."

"Okay, Joy, here we are, and we're

listening. Now what makes you think that the time capsule is buried around here?" asked Ms. Hotchkiss.

Amelia Bedelia smiled at her friend. She knew that whatever Joy said would be amazing.

"It's like a figuring out a word problem in math," said Joy. "The words matter as much as the numbers. When we heard that the time capsule was buried near the

oak tree, everyone assumed it was the big oak tree in front of our school. Not the one behind the school. Not the really old one that died right after they built our school. Now all that is left of that tree is this stump. But maybe this was the only oak tree around here when they buried the time capsule."

Mrs. Roman was nodding the whole time Joy was speaking.

"Then Amelia Bedelia told us that Pete from Pete's Diner is the great-grandson of the first principal," said Joy. "He told Amelia Bedelia about how his great-

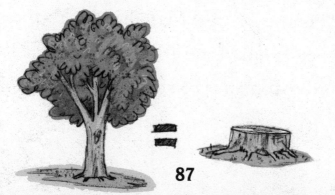

87

grandfather loved trees and felt really bad about the oak tree dying."

Ms. Hotchkiss, Mrs. Roman, and Mrs. Shauk were amazed to learn about Pete's connection to the school.

"Astonishing!" said Ms. Hotchkiss. "Mrs. Roman, please send Pete a VIP invitation to our one hundredth birthday celebration!"

"So I think that the time capsule will be due north of this stump, like Principal Hoffman's letter says," said Joy. "Probably not too far away."

"Penny, go to Ms. Garcia in the science room," said Mrs. Roman. "Tell her you're on a mission for Ms. Hotchkiss, and ask to borrow a compass that shows directions. And Wade, go borrow some shovels—anything we can dig with—from Mr. Jack. Tell him you're on a mission for Ms. Hotchkiss too!"

When Penny raced back with the compass, Joy set it right in the middle of the stump. The magnetic arrow swung back and forth. Joy waited until it had settled down. Once it stopped moving,

the arrow was pointing north.

"I know! We should make a line from the stump to the north," said Clay. "That way we'll know the area where the time capsule is probably buried."

"Great idea!" said Joy. "Amelia Bedelia, please move one step to the right."

Amelia Bedelia took a step, but in the wrong direction.

"I meant to your right," said Joy.

"Right!" said Amelia Bedelia. "I like being right."

"More to the right," said Joy. "You're not right enough."

"Does that make me wrong?" asked Amelia Bedelia.

Joy grabbed Amelia Bedelia's hand and

pulled her behind Holly and Penny. Soon
Mrs. Shauk's students were arranged in a

long line northward from the stump.
Mr. Jack and Wade passed out shovels
and trowels and scoops and spades, and
everyone started to dig.

"I keep hitting rock,"
said Amelia Bedelia.

"Me too," said Joy.

"I think I'm hitting that rock over here," said Skip.

"I'm hitting the same rock over here," said Rose.

"It is hard, but I don't think it's a rock," said Cliff.

Amelia Bedelia and Joy got down on their hands and knees and started clearing away the dirt.

The shovel brigade uncovered what looked like a big stone lid.

"Oh, I think this is it!" said Mrs. Roman. "How exciting!"

"Okay, let's cover it back up now," said Ms. Hotchkiss.

"Why?" asked Amelia Bedelia. "We just uncovered it!" She looked around at her friends. Everyone was shocked!

"Don't you want to see what's in it?" asked Clay, asking the question they were all thinking.

"More than anyone," said Ms. Hotchkiss. "But it can wait until our celebration, when all our students are together and when the newspaper reporters and television crews will be here. That way, we can share our discovery with the whole community."

"That's why you are the principal," said Mrs. Roman. "I just want to go back in time right now."

Amelia Bedelia couldn't agree more. She was so curious!

Everyone dumped a shovelful of dirt back into the hole they had just dug.

"Well, at least it will be easier to dig it up at the celebration," said Wade, mournfully.

Chapter 10

Watch Out . . .

Oak Tree Elementary was finally one hundred years old! It was the perfect day for a party. The air was crisp and clear

and the sun shone on the school building, making it look like a giant cake. The television crew and newspaper reporters arrived early to get set up, and students and parents started arriving, too. Many families brought their dogs. Amelia Bedelia's dog, Finally, was all decked out in ribbons and balloons. Everyone gathered first near the old oak stump for the official kickoff of the centennial celebration.

Amelia Bedelia and her friends were put in charge of digging up the time capsule. After all, they knew exactly where it was, and having practiced once, they uncovered it again

in no time. The hardest part was prying up the stone lid and lifting it off the small vault that held the time capsule. Luckily, Mr. Jack had a crowbar just right for the occasion.

Inside the vault was a metal container about the size of a toolbox. Other than some small rust spots, the time capsule looked like it was in good shape. That meant that the contents would probably have been preserved.

To the sound of hooting and whistling and applause, Amelia Bedelia and Joy lifted the capsule out of the vault and set it gently on the stump table.

Suddenly there was a commotion in the crowd.

At first, Amelia Bedelia did not recognize Pete. She was used to seeing him in a white apron, day in and day out, behind the counter at his diner. She never expected to see him in a blue blazer and a flowered bow tie. He approached the stump and smiled at Amelia Bedelia.

"Hi, Pete!" said Amelia Bedelia.

"Here is our VIP," said Ms. Hotchkiss.

"He sure is. A Very Important Pete," said Amelia Bedelia.

"I clean up pretty well, don't I?" said Pete.

"It took a ton of work," said Doris, smiling as she walked up behind him.

"Pete, we invite you to officially open the time capsule, since it was your great-grandfather who closed it one hundred years ago," said Ms. Hotchkiss.

"Thank you. This is quite an honor," Pete said. "I open this time capsule in the name of Mr. Peter Hoffman, my wonderful great-grandfather and the first principal of our favorite school, Oak

Tree Elementary!" Pete lifted the lid and laughed.

"It didn't even squeak," he said. "I would have after one hundred years!"

He began lifting out items he found inside. There were some games that the students had probably contributed. And photographs of the teachers and the kids, and a fancy pen.

There was a menu from a restaurant. Amelia Bedelia looked over the selections and added up the prices. "Wow," she said. "It would be hard to spend more than a dollar for lunch!"

An issue of the local newspaper was rolled up and tied with string in three places. Ms. Hotchkiss handed it to

Mr. B, the school librarian. He unrolled it and spread the sections out on a nearby picnic table. "Let's see what was happening one hundred years ago," said Mr. B.

Cliff read the sports page. "The 1920 World Series had just ended. The Brooklyn Dodgers lost to Cleveland. Listen to this: 'The New York Yankees are still happy with getting Babe Ruth in a trade from the Boston Red Sox. The Yankees expect he's going to do great things.'" Cliff shook his head.

Joy was shaking her head, too, but for a different reason.

"Guess what happened in 1920!"

GEORGE HERMAN
(BABE) RUTH

BIG LEAGUE CHEWING GUM

DAILY MIRROR

August 26, 1920

WOMEN WIN RIGHT TO VOTE IN

SUFFRAGETTE VICTORY

19th Amendment Ratified

she said. "They added the Nineteenth Amendment to the Constitution!"

"Whoopee! Who cares? Sounds so boring," said Clay. "I want to read about cars."

"But it gave women the right to vote," said Joy.

"What! That's crazy," said Dawn. "Didn't we always have it?"

"You mean a hundred years ago, we couldn't vote?" said Rose.

"Ah, the good old days," said Wade. "Our country has gone downhill ever since you got to vote." He was laughing as he took off running.

The Call-Chronicle-Examiner

DUKE KAHANAMOKU

"Come back here, Wade, so we can vote you out of our class!" said Heather.

"Isn't it strange how we think things were always as they are today?" said Mrs. Shauk. "It's easy to forget how much has changed and how much will change."

Pete had just pulled something out of the capsule. It was small and wrapped carefully.

"What could this be?" asked Pete. "It sure is heavy."

Pete unwrapped the object with care. He began to shake when he realized what he was holding. "This is my great-grandfather's watch!" he said. He pressed a little button and the lid sprang open, revealing a face decorated with Roman numerals. Two words were engraved in fancy script on the inside.

"Tempus fugit," read Pete. "I can't believe I am holding something my great-grandfather used every day."

Chapter 11

B
~~D~~-Day

Amelia Bedelia found her parents and Finally and took them through the school lobby to show them the things that had started the search for the time capsule. The framed photograph that had fallen in the school office had been repaired and looked better than ever.

Amelia Bedelia studied the smiling faces and wondered who had put the bag of marbles in the time capsule. The letter from the first principal to the current principal had been framed and was also on display in the trophy case. Amelia Bedelia showed it to her parents and then pointed to Peter Hoffman, Pete's great-grandfather, in the photograph.

"I see the resemblance," said her mother.

"That's amazing!" said her father. "Sometimes accidents really do lead to surprising discoveries."

Then Amelia Bedelia and her parents went back outside to help with the

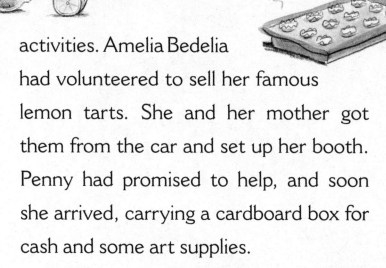

activities. Amelia Bedelia had volunteered to sell her famous lemon tarts. She and her mother got them from the car and set up her booth. Penny had promised to help, and soon she arrived, carrying a cardboard box for cash and some art supplies.

"Oh, no!" said Amelia Bedelia. "I forgot to make a sign." She began arranging the lemon tarts in the shape of a giant letter L that was six tarts wide.

"That L looks yummy," said Penny. She drew a sign that read EMON and propped it up next to the giant letter L to spell LEMON.

"Thanks!" said Amelia Bedelia. "Let's open for business!"

Awoooo! Amelia Bedelia's dog, Finally, spoke up from under a bush next to Amelia Bedelia's booth. Finally had to be wherever Amelia Bedelia's lemon tarts were, because she loved them so much. Too much!

Finally was not the only dog who felt that way about lemon tarts. Most of the dogs in town thought that Amelia

Bedelia's lemon tarts
were spectacular. Most
people did, too.

"Poor Finally!" said
Penny. "Can I save her one tiny little tart
to try?"

Amelia Bedelia nodded and passed one
to Penny. "I always make a special one for
her," she said. "Tiny but tart!"

Penny handled the money, and Amelia
Bedelia served up her lemon tarts to happy
customers. She had to keep rearranging
the tarts into a capital L shape. An hour
later, she only had enough tarts to make a
little *l* shape. After the last two tarts were
sold, Amelia Bedelia and Penny closed the

booth and took off to join in the festivities. Right away, they ran into Rose.

"Check out this picture of me from a hundred years ago!" said Rose, showing them a photograph of her, Heather, and Daisy wearing old-fashioned dresses.

"Wow! You guys look like you stepped out of that photograph in the lobby," said Penny.

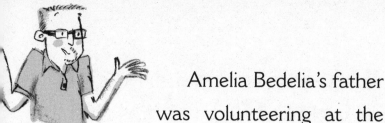 Amelia Bedelia's father was volunteering at the photo booth. While Amelia Bedelia and Penny sorted through the big box of costumes from the 1920s, he explained how he had come to be friends with the photographer.

"We once did a magazine ad for a cookie that was supposed to be baked with real old-fashioned goodness," said Amelia Bedelia's father. "So we made the whole photograph, including the cookie, look like it was from another time!"

"Did people buy a lot of cookies after that?" said Dawn.

"Uhhhhh . . . no. Unfortunately the cookies that looked like they were from another time tasted even older!"

Amelia Bedelia chose a dress that was covered with feathers, and Penny wore a shawl with a long fringe and an even longer pearl necklace. Amelia Bedelia and Penny were very happy with their photographs.

"You two look like true flappers!" said Amelia Bedelia's father.

Amelia Bedelia flapped her arms, and Penny joined in. They fell on the ground laughing.

"Have you seen Mom?" asked Amelia Bedelia as she finally caught her breath.

"I saw her heading that way," said her father, pointing at a table loaded with plants.

Amelia Bedelia and Penny took off their costumes, then waded through the big crowd around the plant table. Amelia Bedelia was certain that her mom was there someplace. Amelia Bedelia's mother adored plants and gardening.

The plant table was covered with little kits labeled:

FOR SALE!

OAK TREE ELEMENTARY KIT

GROW YOUR OWN TREE

WITH AN ACORN FROM OUR TREE!

Each kit included a paper cup filled with soil and a baby oak tree sprouting from an acorn that had fallen off the school's oak tree. The school's motto, MIGHTY OAKS FROM LITTLE ACORNS GROW, was written in fancy writing on each cup.

Just then, someone jumped on Amelia Bedelia and Penny from behind.

Mighty oaks from little acorns grow

"Clay, cut it out!" said Penny.

"Clay, don't do that!" said Amelia Bedelia.

"You like my big idea for getting rid of our millions of acorns?" asked Clay.

"Very smart," said Amelia Bedelia, looking around. "I'm definitely going to buy one as soon as I find my mother."

Amelia Bedelia spotted a beautiful tent next to the plant table. From inside, a whispery voice with a French accent called out to her.

"Are you lost, little girl?"

Before Amelia Bedelia could answer, a mysterious figure emerged. She was a little shorter than Amelia Bedelia, and she was wearing a long purple dress with a bright pink velvet top and lots of eye makeup. Her mass of curly red hair was held back by a sparkly clip with a big flower on it. Her long black fingernails toyed with the large beads of her necklace, and her many bracelets clinked and clanked together.

"Tell Madame Brenda, ma petite. For whom are you searching? A friend? A boyfriend, perhaps?"

"Boyfriend? *Ewwwwww!* GROSS!" said Amelia Bedelia. "I'm looking for my mother."

Madame Brenda put her hands up to the side of her head. She closed her eyes and began rubbing her temples.

"I am receiving signals from a long-ago world. Does the name Finally mean anything to you?"

"Yes!" said Amelia Bedelia. "That's my dog."

"I see ze petite chien Finally walking with your mère," said Madame Brenda,

opening her eyes. "And here they are!"

Just then, Finally barked. She raced up to Amelia Bedelia, wiggling and straining at her leash as Amelia Bedelia's mother tried to hold her back.

"Finally met a pony named Queenie, and I believe she got a little taste of some cotton candy," said Amelia Bedelia's mother. "It took me a while to track her down!"

"Mom, Madame Brenda can predict the future," said Amelia Bedelia. She knelt down next to Finally and tickled her chin.

"Madame Brenda loves to solve all kinds of mysteries," said Madame Brenda. "Especially the history mysteries."

"Hey, wait a minute," said Amelia Bedelia. "We only know one expert history mystery solver at Oak Tree . . . and our friend is about your size!" Amelia Bedelia reached out and grabbed the giant flower from Madame Brenda's head, causing her curly red hair to slide off and hit the ground. Amelia Bedelia laughed.

"Joy! Is that really you?" asked Penny, laughing, too.

Tears of laughter made Joy's makeup run, leaving black streaks down her face.

"You're such a great actor, Joy!" said Amelia Bedelia.

"I have a prediction," said Amelia Bedelia's mother. "Another ceremony is about to take place. Ms. Hotchkiss is getting ready to bury a new time capsule, to be opened one hundred years from today. Let's go watch!"

Chapter 12

. . . Watch In

Amelia Bedelia, Penny, and Joy raced to the student lounge. Kids and parents and teachers were gathered around the stump table, eating ice cream and cotton candy and buzzing like bees.

Mr. Jack held up a two-foot length of white plastic pipe that was a foot in diameter. "This was left over from an odd job I did. It's perfect for storing something. I even glued a cap on the end." He handed it to Mrs. Roman. "Put whatever you want to save in it. Then I'll glue another cap on the other end to seal it."

"Then how do we open it?" asked Wade.

"No one has to worry about that for one hundred years," said Clay. "I'm sure someone in the future will be able to figure it out."

The students of Oak Tree Elementary lined up to put things into the time capsule. Some put in whatever they had in their pockets, such as coins or pens. Others had written long letters. There were a few acorns. Rose put in her favorite book.

"That had better not be a library book," said Mr. B. "You don't want your great-grandchildren to have to pay the fine on a book that is one hundred years overdue."

"This is in honor of you, Mrs. Shauk," said Angel as she and Cliff approached

the stump carrying something. "We are sure that one hundred years from now, kids will still be talking about you."

"We figured that if Roman numerals have lasted this long, then people one hundred years in the future would understand this message," said Cliff. He held up a sign that looked like a license plate.

SHLK IZ GR8

For once Mrs. Shauk had trouble seeing. Her hawk-like eyes were brimming with tears. She hugged Angel and Cliff. "You are all great. This is for everyone at Oak Tree Elementary," said Mrs. Shauk. She held her sign for a minute, then put it in the time capsule.

"Last call," said Ms. Hotchkiss, waving her feathered cap. "Anyone else want to contribute something?"

"Don't seal it yet," said Pete. He came forward and took out his great-grandfather's pocket watch. He held it up for all to see. It sparkled like it was brand-new, reflecting the light as it dangled from its gold chain.

"My great-grandfather devoted his life to the future of this city. He thought that the best way to ensure a bright future was with education. Every generation climbs upon the shoulders of the one that came before, trying to see into the future. My great-grandfather helped many little acorns grow into mighty oaks. One hundred years ago, he contributed his most prized possession to the future. Today, I would like to do the same, to honor his memory and his faith in us."

People were applauding Pete long after he wrapped up the watch in its original covering and carefully placed it in the time capsule. Clay's father applied glue to the end of the pipe, and Ms. Hotchkiss was given the honor of putting on the cap to seal it. Then Clay's father handed it to Dawn and Cliff to put into its stone vault by the student lounge and the stump.

Amelia Bedelia was standing next to Clay, whispering back and forth during the ceremony.

"This feels like a funeral," said Clay. "A bunch of people standing around watching a burial."

"Remember when we buried that pet gecko in my backyard?" said Amelia Bedelia.

"I sure do," said Clay. "I was the one who defrosted him, after months in the freezer."

"What was its name?" said Amelia Bedelia.

"Roger," whispered Clay.

"No, that was the owner," said Amelia Bedelia.

They were quiet until the name popped into both of their heads at the same time.

"Georgie!" they said loudly.

$Shhhhh!!$

"SHHHHHHH!" said Mrs. Shauk. glancing behind her to catch who was talking.

Amelia Bedelia looked around, trying to memorize the faces of her friends and the people in her hometown. It was dawning on her that no one there today would be around for the two hundredth birthday celebration to open their time capsule. Not her teachers, not her parents, not Finally, and probably not her.

Amelia Bedelia was happy that she had taken the time to write a note and put it in the time capsule. She'd written it in cursive, then printed it too, in case the people in 2120 couldn't read cursive.

To the students of Oak Tree Elementary,

There is nothing I can do to impress
you. There is no invention or technology
that will not be out of date in one
trying to predict
hundred
e kind and
to make the

iend,

a Bedelia

To the students of Oak Tree
                        Elementary,

There is nothing I can do
to impress you.   There is no
invention or technology I have
that will not be out of date
in one hundred years. Instead
of trying to predict what the
world will be like in one
hundred years, I promise
that I will be kind and
helpful and work REALLY
           hard to make the
♡ world better for -☺-
          the future.

                    Your friend,
                    Amelia Bedelia

As the ceremony came to a close, Amelia Bedelia and her friends grabbed shovels and helped Mr. Jack bury their time capsule back in the stone vault.

"I know what we need!" said Joy, once they had finished piling up the dirt and stamping it down. "Ice cream!"

Amelia Bedelia laughed. "That is a date!"

Amelia Bedelia

& FRIENDS

The Cat's Meow

Hi!
Turn the page
for a special
sneak peek
at my next
adventure!

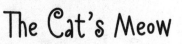

Amelia Bedelia & FRIENDS

The Cat's Meow

by Herman Parish   pictures by Lynne Avril

Chapter 1

If at First You Don't Succeed

"Remember, people!" said Ms. Garcia, Amelia Bedelia's science teacher at Oak Tree Elementary. "All great inventors think outside the box!"

Amelia Bedelia looked at her friend Joy and shrugged. Teachers were always telling them to think outside the box.

Amelia Bedelia rarely stood

in a box to think, and neither did any of her friends. But Amelia Bedelia had also never invented anything famous—at least not yet. Not a lightbulb, like Thomas Edison . . . or shampoo made out of peanuts, like George Washington Carver . . . or a chocolate chip cookie, like Ruth Wakefield . . . or even a pair of earmuffs, like Chester Greenwood.

"An inventor starts with a problem and then finds a solution that doesn't already exist," Ms. Garcia continued. "So, let's think about that for a minute. What is a problem that you would like to solve?"

Finally is top dog!

Amelia Bedelia loves Finally, her one and only pup! They have tons of fun together. And that isn't some shaggy dog story!

A dog and pony show

It's a dog's life

Like a dog with a bone

As sick as a dog

It's a dog's life

It's raining cats and dogs

The dog ate my homework

Two Ways to Say It
By Amelia Bedelia

"Don't get on
her bad side."

"Don't make
her mad at you."

"Are you a lucky duck
or a dead duck?"

"Are you super lucky
or in big trouble?"

"They blew up the photo."

"They enlarged the photo."

"Try not to get winded."

"Try not to get tired
and breathless."

"Mr. Jack carried the
package single-handedly."

"Mr. Jack carried
the package by himself."

138

"Beat the clock!"

"Get something done before the deadline."

"Anything earth-shattering happen today?"

"Did anything really surprising and interesting happen?"

"That's a huge feather in your cap!"

"Congratulations! You did something amazing!"

"The tarts are the hottest thing on the menu."

"The tarts are the most popular thing we sell."

"My french fries are on the house."

"I didn't pay for my french fries—they're free!"

139

The Amelia Bedelia Chapter Books

With Amelia Bedelia, anything can happen!

Amelia Bedelia wants a new bike—a brand-new, shiny, beautiful, fast bike. A bike like that is really expensive and will cost an arm and a leg!

Amelia Bedelia is getting a puppy—a sweet, adorable, loyal, friendly puppy!

Have you read them all?

Amelia Bedelia is hitting the road. Where is she going? It's a surprise!

Amelia Bedelia is going to build a zoo in her backyard. Better yet, she is going to invite all her friends to bring their pets and help plan the exhibits and rides.

Amelia Bedelia usually loves recess, but one day she doesn't get picked for a team and she begins to have second thoughts about sports.

Amelia Bedelia and her friends are determined to find a cool clubhouse for their new club.

Amelia Bedelia is so excited to be spending her vacation at the beach! But one night, she sees her cousin sneaking out the window. Where is he going?

New steps inspire Amelia Bedelia and her dance school classmates to dance up a storm!

What does Amelia Bedelia want to be when she grows up? Turns out, the sky's the limit!

When disaster strikes and threatens to ruin her aunt's wedding, it's up to Amelia Bedelia to make sure Aunt Mary and Bob tie the knot!

An overlap camp is not Amelia Bedelia's idea of fun—especially not *this* camp, which sounds as though it's super boring and rustic. What Amelia Bedelia needs is a new plan, fast!

11

Amelia Bedelia
Makes a Splash

by Herman Parish • pictures by Lynne Avril

12

Amelia
Bedelia
Digs In

by Herman Parish • pictures by Lynne Avril

Amelia Bedelia and her parents are heading to the shore for summer vacation and that means sailing, surfing, eating a ton of ice cream, and just hanging out. And what about the mystery of the buried treasure?

145

Introducing...
Amelia Bedelia
& FRIENDS

Amelia Bedelia +
Good Friends =
Super Fun Stories
to Read and Share

Amelia Bedelia and her friends celebrate their school's birthday.

Amelia Bedelia and her friends discover a stray kitten on the playground!

Amelia Bedelia and her friends take a school trip to the Middle Ages that is as different as knight and day.

Coming soon . . .

Amelia Bedelia wants to bury
her own personal time capsule in her
backyard. Here are the things she'll put
in it for future friends to find. Each item
makes her remember a special friend,
relative, or fun adventure!

1. Her lemon tart recipe

2. A picture of Finally

3. A postcard from
   Lake Largemouth

4. Fuzzy slippers

5. A whistle

6. A picture of Minsk and Timbuktu

7. A copy of *Treasure Island*

8. Ballet slippers

9. A roll of pennies

10. A rope tied in a knot

11. A piece of flint

flint

12. A shell from the shore

What would you put in your time capsule?